THE WHITE NOTEBOOK

THE WHITE NOTEBOOK

By ANDRE GIDE

*Translated and with an Introduction
by Wade Baskin*

THE CITADEL PRESS
New York

FIRST PAPERBOUND EDITION 1965

PUBLISHED BY THE CITADEL PRESS
222 PARK AVENUE SOUTH, NEW YORK 3, N. Y.
COPYRIGHT 1964 BY PHILOSOPHICAL LIBRARY, INC.
LIBRARY OF CONGRESS CATALOG CARD NUMBER 64-16975
MANUFACTURED IN THE UNITED STATES OF AMERICA

INTRODUCTION

"It was not only my first work, it was my summation," wrote André Gide in *If It Die* (1926), and the truth of his statement concerning *The Notebooks of André Walter* was borne out by his intimate writings, some of them not published until after his death. *The White Notebook* and its Manichean twin *The Black Notebook* were published in one volume in 1891 (the author was supposed to have died after asking a friend to decide whether or not the notebooks should be published posthumously). Gide had misgivings about allowing the *Notebooks* to be reprinted later (1930) as one of his *Representative Works*, but as he noted in a preface, his concern was purely aesthetic and in the early work he probably had put most of himself. Those who have read *Et nunc manet in te*, published in 1951, the year of his death, will agree.

Gide once complained that La Bruyère painted men as they were but without telling us how they became what they were. Gide's works are one sustained attempt to understand and explain himself. *The White Notebook*, his first experiment in self-analysis through the medium of art and the first stage in his quest for authenticity, is a projection onto the printed page of the inner conflicts of

André Walter, the ill-starred double of André Gide. Walter's passions and conflicts, his temptations and anguish, his eventual triumph over demoniac forces through a mystic, ideal love yield a portrait of Gide's adolescent ego. The portait suggests the direction of his subsequent development.

For months he had nurtured the notion of writing the *Notebooks,* but not until late spring in 1890 did he begin to work systematically on the project. At that time he was twenty and felt not only that the crisis which he was attempting to depict was typical but also that the world was waiting for his contribution. He isolated himself from the world by moving into a chalet not far from the famed Carthusian monastery near Grenoble in southeastern France. When he set out in May, 1890, he was convinced that in order to complete his work he must find seclusion.

Not since the death of his father ten years earlier had he been separated from his mother for as long as twenty-four hours. The letters which he exchanged with her and the notebooks in which he recorded his comments on his readings provide many details concerning the period of the writing of the *Notebooks.*

Because of his admiration for the writings of Flaubert and Goethe, the work originally published as *The Notebooks of André Walter* might well have been assigned another title. Gide vacillated between *Allain* (or *Alain*) and *The New Sentimental Education* in his search for an appropriate title. The influence of Flaubert is also seen in the choice of a Breton hero. Furthermore, Gide had read *The Sorrows of Young Werther,* much of it in German, and was certainly aware of parallels between Goethe's early semi-autobiographical work and his own. The similarity between the names assigned to the two heroes is striking.

In all probability, however, the writer who most impressed Gide during the period of the composition of *The White Notebook* was neither Flaubert nor Goethe. It was Schopenhauer. *The World as Will and Idea,* which he first read in 1899, produced in Gide a feeling of "ineffable rapture." Years later he wrote that he attributed to Schopenhauer his philosophical outlook and his awareness of a second reality behind the appearance of things as well as his passion for music and poetry. The style of *The World as Will and Idea* appealed to him, as did Schopenhauer's pessimistic analysis of life, his glorification of art as the great source of revelation of the nature of reality, his identification of the will as the source of anguish, his emphasis on the fundamental antagonism between dream and reality, and his advocacy of mortification of the will to live. The influence of Schopenhauer also shows up in the form—or formlessness—of *The White Notebook.*

Like Schopenhauer, Gide found reality illusory and equivocal. For Walter truth is subject to the will (things *become* true). His conflicts are always in the inner life, not in the outer world. Reality is transformed and transcended by his primary vision. When asked late in life whether his wife had served him as the model for Alissa, the heroine of *Strait Is the Gate,* Gide answered, "She *became* Alissa." His reply is characteristic and highly significant. *The White Notebook* sets the pattern of symbolic transformation through which he was to objectify throughout his lifetime the tensions and conflicts that motivated his creativity.

The psychological forces involved in the transformation of his conflicts and tensions are detailed in a recent study by Dr. Jean Delay, *The Youth of André Gide* (abridged and translated by June Guicharnaud, 1963). Dr. Delay diagnoses Gide's neurosis in terms of mother image, narcissism, angelism, etc., and calls attention to his devotion to his mother and to her puritanical code. By her conduct both before and during the period embraced by Walter's notebooks, she interfered with the normal development of Gide's libido and caused him to turn to art as the only means of liberating his demons. Through the process of objectifying his inner tensions and conflicts he managed to escape from reality and enter into the realm of the imagination. Art was for him a means of transcending reality.

It is easy to establish parallels between the creatures of Gide's imagination and the persons who were important in his life. Like André Gide, André Walter is the product of two bloodstreams, two cultures and two temperaments. Like Madeleine, who later became Mme. Gide, Emmanuèle is fearful, withdrawn, in need of André's protection. Like Gide's mother, Walter's mother is pious and imperious, and she tries to prevent the marriage of her son. In both situations André can transcend his situation only by overcoming carnal desire and idealizing his love for both his mother and his companion.

Gide had several reasons for writing the *Notebooks*.

One of these was to enhance his chances of marrying his cousin, Madeleine Rondeaux. It might be well to review the background against which was unfolded the drama of his literary proposal and its part in an even longer drama.

As a child he had manifested an autoeroticism which had caused him to suffer considerable embarrassment and to incur his mother's antipathy. An ambivalent feeling toward his mother was manifested at an early age. He apparently was happier when living away from her than when living with her. After the death of his father, however, he never left her side until the spring when he started to write the *Notebooks*. Shortly after her death in 1895, Gide married.

Gide's mother had opposed the marriage of her son and her niece, Madeleine Rondeaux, and this for several reasons. Aside from the fact that they were first cousins, she felt that her son was too immature and too irresponsible to care for a girl who, though older than he, had suffered much and needed a sense of stability and security which he could not provide. She may also have doubted the sincerity of their love since they had lived for a long time as brother and sister.

Madeleine also had the same valid reasons for rejecting his proposal. Besides, she probably realized that Gide had a false image of her. There is no doubt but that he consistently refused to face the facts, that in his imagination he transformed circumstances, idealized situations, and attributed to her a personality, a psychology, a character which she would scarcely have acknowledged. That the real Madeleine at the beginning of their marriage was not the Alissa in *Strait Is the Gate* is obvious to anyone who has read *Et nunc manet in te* (1951). Unable or unwilling to appreciate the advice of his mother and the decision of his cousin, Gide blamed the former for interfering with his plans and continued his campaign to win the hand of the latter. To retain the love of both, he had to renounce physical possession and build an image that would accommodate both.

His fictional image had to blend the attributes of both mother and cousin. This he accomplished in *The White Notebook* by fusing the remembered image of an older sister who had died with the Emmanuèle who lived in Walter's imagination—all purity, all goodness, all that he envisioned as noblest and best in himself. He had fallen in love with a fictitious entity as inaccessible as the reflection of Narcissus: a projection of his superego. Here the supreme achievement of love would be the annihilation of the body and the freeing of the soul. The bedside scene in which Walter renounces possession of Emmanuèle in favor of a higher union anticipates the supposed relationship of Gide and Madeleine after his marriage to "the only love in my life."

Gide believed not only that his first work was of general interest but also that it would overcome the objections of his mother and the resistance of Madeleine to his proposal. It was to bring glory to him and make everyone concerned realize that his noble, moving declaration of love should be opposed by no one.

The book was published at the author's expense (or

rather his mother's). In a few special copies the name Madeleine was substituted for Emmanuèle. A copy was presented to her with an appropriate inscription and the request that she read it the same night. Her diary shows that she was moved to tears when she finally read it but that she found it too true to life and considered it an invasion of her privacy. Her polite but formal rejection of his proposal hurt him deeply, but he still felt kindly toward her. It would seem that nothing that she had ever said actually gave him grounds for thinking that she wanted to marry him, and that here again the facts were not as he had imagined them.

He could, however, draw some comfort from the attention given his work by critics. Stéphane Mallarmé and Henri de Régnier praised the delicate quality of its style. Maurice Maeterlinck noted that it "eternalized" the struggles of a virtuous soul. Joris-Karl Huysmans and others saw in Walter's plight a new "sickness of the century," or rather of the last half of the century. Rémy de Goncourt hailed the book as the distillation of all the study, dreaming, passion and anguish that make up youth and the author of the anonymous work as a romantic-philosophical disciple of Goethe. The same critic predicted that the author's future work would take a turn in the direction of irony.

Gide lived up to Goncourt's expectations by becoming a master in the use of gentle irony. A blend of irony, humor, parable and narrative genius made it possible for him to sustain a rewarding dialog with readers and himself. Though as an avowed purist he expressed misgivings about *The Notebooks,* he could never divorce aesthetics and ethics. The result is that his dialog is always tinged with ethical considerations. Only a self-imposed morality could enable André Gide—or André Walter, the first typical Gidean hero—to achieve the highest potential of his being.

* * *

I have tried through occasional notes to call attention to significant facts that may be of interest to the reader. In many instances I have borrowed freely from the writings of Dr. Jean Delay. I wish also to express my appreciation to Professor Ralph Behrens, who read the first draft of my translation and made many constructive suggestions, and to the others who have helped me to prepare for publication this edition of Gide's first work: Jim Barnes, James Gamble, Cherry Jeffrey, Pat Livingston, William McCray and Diane Puckett.

WADE BASKIN

SOUTHEASTERN STATE COLLEGE

Wait till your sadness is assuaged, poor soul, wearied by the struggle of yesterday.

Wait.

When tears are shed
cherished hopes will blossom anew.
Now you must sleep.

Lullabies, ballads, barcaroles,
The song of the willows smoothes the cadence.

*   *   *

You must say a good prayer this evening, and you must believe. This you will have forever. No one can take it from you. You will say: *"The Lord is the portion of mine inheritance . . . when my father and my mother forsake me, then the Lord will take me up."*[1]

And then you will sleep. Think no more; bitter days are still too near.

Let memories feed your dreams.

Rest.

---

[1] Gide rightly emphasized in many of his writings the influence of his early puritanical training on his art. According to him, two-thirds of the biblical quotations set down in the first draft of the *Notebooks* were eliminated before publication at the suggestion of his friend, Albert Démarest. (Notes not numbered are supplied by the translator.)

Thursday

Wrote some letters. . . .
I tried to read, to think. . . . Exhaustion soothed my sadness, which now seems but a dream.
Now beneath the trees
The darkness is comforting.

How silent is the night. I am almost afraid to fall asleep. I am alone. Thought emerges from a dark background; the future appears above the dark as a ribbon of space. Nothing distracts me from *my primary vision*. I am this vision and nothing more.[2]

* * *

Some evening, turning back, I shall repeat these words of sorrow; now it sickens me to write. Words are not for these things, not for emotions too pure to be spoken. I am afraid that empty, high-sounding words are blasphemous; hating the words that I have loved too much, I wish to write badly by design. I wish to disrupt harmonies wherever they happen to exist.[3]

Rest in peace, mother. I have been obedient.
My soul still smarts from its dual ordeal, but sadness is giving way to pride of conquest. You knew me well if you thought that by its very excess virtue would entice

---

[2] The primary vision (*la vision commencée*) appears in *Urien's Voyage* as the idea or principle which each of us is to manifest in his own life. This section reflects the influence of Schopenhauer's *The World as Will and Idea* on the young writer.

[3] In a later preface to the *Notebooks* (1930), the author expressed regret over its defects, holding that the writer should always exercise absolute control over his medium.

me. You knew that arduous and challenging paths lure me, that senseless pursuits appeal to me because of my dream, and that a little folly is necessary for the satisfaction of my pride.[4]

You made them all depart in order that you might speak to me alone (it was only a few hours before the end).

"André my child," you said, "I want to die assured." I already knew what you would say to me and had summoned up all my strength. You hastened to speak because you were very tired.

"It would be good for you to leave Emmanuèle. . . . Your affection is fraternal—make no mistake about it. . . . It springs from the life in common that you have been leading. Although she is my niece, do not make me regret having treated her as my own since she became an orphan. I would not wish to allow you complete freedom, for fear that your emotions would mislead you and make the both of you unhappy. Do you understand why? Emmanuèle has already suffered much. I want more than anything else for her to be happy. Do you love her enough to prefer her happiness to yours?"[5]

Then you spoke of T*** who had just responded to the sad news.

---

[4] Gide later condemned the pride that resulted from such a victory. He insisted that he had at first thought it good to struggle, that true wisdom consisted in accepting defeat, in not opposing oneself.

[5] Jean Delay in his monumental work on the early life of Gide (*La Jeunesse d'André Gide,* Gallimard, 1956) maintains that in the foregoing passage the writer reveals for the first time one of the deepest secrets of his psychology: the influence of his mother in preventing his physical union with Madeleine Rondeaux.

"Emmanuèle thinks highly of him," you remarked.
I knew that she did, but I remained silent.
"Have I put too much trust in you, my child?" you continued, "or can I die assured?"
I was exhausted by the recent ordeals.
"Yes, mother," I said, not really understanding but wishing to continue to the end—to hurl myself into the heart of darkness.
I departed. When they summoned me, I saw Emmanuèle near your bed, clasping the hand of T***. We knelt and prayed. My thoughts were confused—then you went to sleep.

After the palliative rites, we had communion together. Emmanuèle was in front of me. I did not look at her. To avoid thinking of her and lapsing into reveries, I repeated: "Since I must lose her, may I at least find Thee again, O Lord. Bless me for following the strait and narrow path."
Then I departed. I came here because I could not rest.[6]

Thursday
I worked in order to keep my mind occupied. It is through work that my mind is revitalized.
I took out all the written pages which recall the past. I want to read them once more, to arrange them, to copy

---
[6] Publication of the *Notebooks* did mark a turning point in the life of the author. It marked the end of his sheltered life of mystic revery and passive introspection and the beginning of an active life of exploration and conquest. Schopenhauer's visionary became the romantic disciple of Goethe.

them, to relive them. I will write some stories based on old memories.

I will turn my thoughts from earlier dreams in order to begin a new life. When memories are set down, my soul will be lighter.[7] I will stop them in their flight. Whatever is not yet forgotten is not entirely dead. I do not wish to leave behind me without even a parting nod the enduring fancies of my youth.

But why try to find reasons to justify a stand already taken, as if by way of an apology? I write because I need to write—and that sums up everything. A stand is weakened by attempted explanations; the act should be spontaneous.

And with revitalized ambition comes a reawakening of the hope of completing *Allain*, the book that I have long dreamed of writing.[8]

20 *April*
The air is so radiant this morning that in spite of myself my soul hopes—and sings, and worships prayerfully.

E però leva su! Vince l'ambascia
Con l'animo che vince ogni battaglia

---

[7] Setting the pattern that was to serve for a lifetime of creative effort, the author abstracts from reality and freely changes details. His mother's words might well have been spoken after the death of Émile Rondeaux, the father of Madeleine (Emmanuèle).

[8] It is significant that the book originally envisioned as *Allain* was finally published as *The Notebooks of André Walter*. The German name suggests of course Goethe's *Werther*, which has a similar theme and which Gide was reading during the period of the composition of the *Notebooks*.

Se col suo grave corpo non s'accascia . . .
E dissi: "Va, ch'i son forte e ardito". . . .[9]

21 *April*

Nothing happens. Always the quiet life—and yet such a turbulent life. Everything happens deep in the soul. Nothing appears on the surface. How can I write about nothing? My thoughts have nothing on which to build, and my persistent passions, offspring of a forgotten past, have imperceptibly reached their peak.[10]

I would fashion a soul, shape it deliberately—a loving soul, a beloved soul, similar to my own—in order that it might understand and yet from such a distance that nothing could ever separate the two. Slowly I would tie such intricate knots, weave such a network of sympathetic bonds, that separation would be impossible and shared patterns would forever keep them side by side.[11]

---

[9] And therefore raise thee up, o'ercome thy panting
With spirit that o'ercometh every battle,
If with its heavy body it sink not. . . .
And said: "Go on, for I am strong and bold."
(Longfellow's translation.)

[10] The tumultuous inner life with its conflicting passions and ideals is an appropriate theme for Gide's first published work. During the period of its composition he expressed the opinion that the crisis depicted in it was of such general interest that others might use it before he completed his work. Later, in his autobiographical *If It Die* (1926), he wrote, "It was not only my first book, it was my summation."

[11] It has been said that Gide's art is a sustained attempt to understand and explain himself. Perhaps *The White Notebook* is a symbolic account of his struggle to free himself from carnal temptations through the mystic, idealized love first experienced in his youth. Delay sees the perfect image which he creates here (an Echo for Narcissus) as the projection of his superego: the embodiment in his love of all those qualities which he holds in high esteem. Jean-Paul Sartre's handling of a similar theme in *Saint-Genêt* (1952) suggests the connection between André Walter's search for a kindred soul and André Gide's predicament.

Monday

We learned everything together. I thought only of joys shared with you, and you took pleasure in following my lead. Your vagabond mind also sought companionship.

First came the Greeks, always our favorites: the *Iliad*, *Prometheus*, *Agamemnon*, *Hippolytus*. And when, knowing the meaning, you wanted to hear the harmony of the lines, I would read:

>................Τενέδοιό τε ἶφι ἀνάσσεις
>Σμινθεῦ............
>   Τέχνον, τί χλαίεις; τίδέ σε φρένας ἵχετο πένθος;;
>Αἴρετέ μου δέμας, ὀρθοῦτε χάρα.
>λέλυμαι μελέων σύνδεσμα, φίλαι.
>Αἴ, Αἴ,
>πῶς ἂν δροσερᾶς ἀπό χρηνῖδος
>χαθαρῶν, ὑδάτων πῶμ' ἀρυσαίμην......

Then came *King Lear*:
Through the sharp hawthorne blows the cold wind. . . .
Shakespeare's dramatic genius fired us with enthusiasm. There were no such thrills in real life.

Words of a Believer had the ring of true prophecy. Later, of course, you found Lamennais' eloquence somewhat trite. I was vexed by your criticism, even though apt, because emotion floods his pages, and emotion is always beautiful.

Then we would go back to childhood readings, first studied in the classical manner with ravishing delight: Pascal, Boussuet . . .[12] Massillon. But instead of the specious

---
[12] Name crossed out. (Gide's note.)

charm of the *Carême* we preferred the word-magic of the *Funeral Orations* of Jansenist sternness. . . .

And so many others still—and all the others.

* * *

Acknowledging our common aspirations, we went on to Vigny, Baudelaire—to Flaubert, the friend long anticipated![13] We marveled at his masterful rhythm. The rhetorical subtleties of the Goncourts sharpened our minds; Stendhal made them more receptive, more critical. . . .[14]

ΣΥΜΠΑΘΕΙΝ: to suffer together, to be impassioned together.

I saw the Sphinx as it fled toward Libya; like a jackal it galloped along.

Loudly I declaimed it, developing first the line and then emphasizing the dactyl. Both of us trembled to the majestic cadences.

You wrote that T*** reread to us the other evening Du Camp and Flaubert's *Eastern Voyage*. He recited for us the rhythmical apostrophe that we love, but whether he reads it for us or I read it myself, the voice that I hear is always yours.

* * *

---

[13] The notebooks in which Gide recorded his readings show that he read the writers mentioned here during the period of the composition of *The White Notebook*. Gustave Flaubert deserves special mention since he influenced Gide's aesthetics and caused him to consider titling his first book *The New Sentimental Education*. (Flaubert's *Sentimental Education* was inspired in part by personal reminiscences, notably those of his unhappy love affair, at sixteen, with an older woman who later lost her mind.)

[14] Word missing. (Gide's note.)

We were still reading from the *Temptation*:[15]

> *O Fantasy, bear me away on your wings to mitigate my sorrow . . . Egypt! Egypt! The shoulders of your great motionless Gods have been bleached by bird-droppings, and the wind that passes over the desert stirs the ashes of your dead! . . . Spring will return no more, O eternal Mother!*
> *. . . You cannot imagine the long journey that we have taken. The green courier's onagers died of exhaustion. . . .*

And we read much more until finally we tired of repeating the passages, of bringing out all their harmony, of letting the pulsating rhythms echo back and forth until the refrain clung to the lips of one of us and was intelligible to the other—in the absence of speech.

* * *

I related to you my aspirations; you smiled, trying your best to seem incredulous.

"And the book that I have been dreaming of writing," I told you, "will be called ALLAIN."

Allain, the book that I dreamed of writing! I saw it as a melancholy and romantic work at first, when with the stirring of my senses I roamed the forests in search of solitude and was prey to unknown anxieties; when the

---

[15] *The Temptation of Saint Anthony*, a romantic adaptation of an old Christian legend, pictures the hermit in the desert, tempted by sensual pleasures and secret intellectual delights but victorious in his struggle to remain virtuous.

song of the wind in the swaying pines seemed to give voice to my resurgent yearnings; when I wept over falling leaves, over setting suns, over vanishing streams of water; and when at the sound of the sea I would lapse into a day of revery. Then I saw it as metaphysical and profound when my mind began to harbor doubts—childish doubts, perhaps, but doubts that caused me considerable anxiety. There cannot be two ways of doubting.[16]

At the outset I saw the book as a character sketch with neither episodes nor plot.

Then I had the notion of studying our love rather than portraying a character who declaimed about such things, and of recreating the intensity and immediacy of our experience.[17]

25 April

They will never understand this book, those who search for happiness. The soul remains unsatisfied; it falls asleep amid happy surroundings. It becomes inert rather than alert. The soul should remain alert, active. It should find happiness not in HAPPINESS but in the awareness of its violent activity.

It follows that sorrow is to be preferred over joy, for it quickens the soul; when it does not vanquish it stimu-

---

[16] Gide wrote that Schopenhauer was responsible for his alternating periods of anguish and ecstasy, for his awareness of a second reality behind the visible one, and for his passion for poetry and music.

[17] Pierre Louis warned Gide against undertaking an autobiographical work at the age of twenty and cited Goethe's regret over the shortcomings of *Werther* as proof that such an undertaking should come toward middle age. Ironically, structural integrity and variety of detail, the two elements advocated by Louis, are missing from the *Notebooks*.

lates. It causes suffering, but pride of undaunted living compensates for minor lapses. Supreme arrogance is the mark of intense living. I would not exchange the intense life for any other; I have lived several lives, and the least of these was the real one.[18]

My life will be more intense, my soul more vigilant. My listless soul will no longer lament but will rejoice in its nobility.

* * *

The thrill, both moral and physical, that grips you at the sight of sublime things, the thrill at first considered unique by each of us with the result that neither mentioned it to the other—what joy when we discovered that it was the same in both of us! It was an overwhelming emotion. What joy, afterwards, to experience it together as we read; it seemed to unite us in the same surge of enthusiasm. And the same thrill was soon felt by each of us through the other, in the other; with our hands joined and our bodies in close contact, we became inseparably one.

And when we read and my voice alternately rose and fell, I knew the sounds and the passages which we loved and which would make us both quiver with delight.

Fools! Nor would you have believed me . . .
Scamander, Meander, beloved of the Priamides.

---

[18] This passage invites comparison of André Walter and his feminine counterpart, Alissa, in *Strait Is the Gate* (1909). She epitomizes the same ideal and mystical love. Afraid of physical love, she longs for an impossible happiness, for perfect Love, for God.

The names alone, the Greek names with their long endings, awakened in us such magnificent memories that each burst of sound aroused latent feelings of exaltation.

One summer evening we were returning from H***. We had been left alone on top of the carriage. The others were inside. The route was long and night was coming on rapidly. We wrapped around us a common shawl; our cheeks almost touched.

"I have brought along the Gospel," I said to her. "If you wish, we can read together while there is still some light."

"Read," said Emmanuèle.[19]

After I had finished reading to her, I asked: "Shall we pray together?"

"No," she answered. "Let's pray silently. Otherwise we would think of ourselves rather than of God."

We fell silent, but I was still thinking about you.

Night had fallen. "What are you thinking about?" she asked. And I recited:

Friendly dawn sleeps in the valley....

---

[19] Emmanuèle is the fictional name of Madeleine Rondeaux, who appears under a different name in many other works. Significant details of her life before and after she became Mme. André Gide have been related in subsequent works, notably *If It Die, Strait Is the Gate* and *Et nunc manet in te* (1951). These include the infidelity and divorce of her mother, the death of her father, and her unconsummated marriage together with the suffering, privation and shame which she endured for her husband's sake. In Gide's imagination Emmanuèle was transformed, idealized, ennobled, imbued with the very qualities he would like to have attributed to himself.

Then it was her turn:

*Farewell, leisurely voyages, sounds heard from afar.
Laughter of the passer-by, screeching of axle-tree,
Unexpected turns along irregular slopes,
A friend rediscovered, hours whiled away,
Hope of arriving late in some wilderness....*

Then mine again:

*But you, indolent traveler, will you not
Put your head on my shoulder and dream?*

And because it was growing late, both of us fell asleep, lost in dreams, our bodies in close contact, our hands joined....

... Then suddenly a brutal awakening as if from a dream: we had run into a wagon on the dark road. We heard voices and the rattling of chains but saw nothing. We heard the barking of dogs and noticed a faint light outlined against the panes of a nearby farmhouse—or so we thought. Trembling a little, we drew even closer to each other, put our trust in each other.

*Dreaming of black, heavy wagons that noisily by night
Pass by the thresholds of farms
   And cause the dogs to bark in the dark.*

While we slept the lanterns had been lighted. We watched with amusement for the indistinct shapes of bushes to leap from the shadows as we passed by. We looked for known shapes which would tell us how far we had to travel.

Then the sound of footsteps: a belated traveler suddenly illuminated by a gust of light. And as the rays moved on through the darkness they silhouetted the shadows of night butterflies as they approached and collided with the panes in the lanterns.

I recall the warmer air that caressed our brows as we crossed empty fields and smelled the perfume of damp plowed ground. We listened to the singing of the frogs. . . .

Then at last the arrival, laughter once again, the hearth, the lamp and warmth-giving tea. But both of us kept in our souls the memory of a deeper intimacy.

Not the landscape itself, not the emotion caused by the landscape. The setting of vanished suns, the peacefulness of dusk still floods my soul. O the peacefulness of beams of light on the plain!

Soon after the meal we ran to the pond; it became iridescent as it reflected the clouds.

At L*** M***, you remember, we would go at nightfall as far as the menhirs. Belated harvesters sang to each other as they made their way homeward on burdened carts; then their songs faded away in the distance. Crickets chirped in fields of wheat.

For a long time we would watch the darkness spread across the violet sea and rise like a tide from the depths of valleys, gradually blotting out all shapes. One by one on distant slopes lighthouses began to glow, and one by one in the distant sky the stars grew brighter. As we made our way homeward, Venus twinkled, caressing our eyes with her friendly light. . . .

And the night was descending on our ravished souls.[20]

In the morning you attended to your housekeeping chores. I watched as you passed through the long corridors in your white apron; I waited for you on the stairway, at the kitchen doors; I enjoyed helping you and seeing you at work; together we went up to the huge linen-room—and sometimes while you put away the linen I followed you about, reading a selection previously begun.

Then I called you Martha, for you were *preoccupied with many things.*

But in the evening it was again Mary, for after you were freed from the cares of the day, you again became contemplative.

. . . You had been assigned to Lucie's room.[21] It seemed

---

[20] The choice of Brittany as the setting may have resulted from Gide's admiration for Flaubert. The interplay of setting, race, and religion may reflect the thinking of Hippolyte Taine, whose works were of especial interest to him during the period of the composition of the *Notebooks*. An interesting parallel between the two Andrés can be established on the basis of Taine's three great factors (Race, Environment and Epoch): Walter's Breton mother was a Catholic, his Saxon father a Protestant; Gide's Norman mother came from a Catholic family, and his Protestant father traced his ancestry to Languedoc; both were the product of two bloodstreams, two regions and two faiths; the anguish of both was caused by the interplay of Taine's three factors.

[21] Lucie was an older sister whom André Walter had lost in 1885. (Gide's note.)

that the dear departed one had not completely vacated it. When you moved in, the things that had once been hers seemed to recognize her and to come to life again. I saw everything as it had once been: the table, the books, the large curtains that darkened the bed, the chair where I came to read, the vase with the flowers that I had picked for you. . . . In the midst of all that you seemed to be reliving a former life, a life that had already been lived. Particles of *her* memory surrounded you, making you more pensive. In the evening I saw *her* profile in the blurred silhouette of your bowed head, and your voice reminded me of her whenever you spoke. And soon both of your images became blurred in my memory.[22]

They had faith in us and we in each other; we had adjoining rooms.

Do you remember the lovely evening when I returned to you after we had said good night to them?

(August, 1887)

"Sleep claims all that surrounds us and through the window opened to the stars on this summer night come the sporadic cries of nocturnal birds or the rustling of moist leaves driven by puffs of wind, as soft as a lover's whispered words.

"We are alone in your room, overcome by tenderness

---
[22] The influence of the older sister illustrates Gide's technique of abstracting and reinterpreting reality in terms of his own psychology. It has been suggested that the older sister is identified with Gide's mother —the symbol of purity and the one who keeps Emmanuèle (Madeleine) and André physically apart even as she makes possible their mystical union.

and passion. In the caress of the air, in the smell of hay, of lime-trees, of roses; in the mystery of the hour, in the calm of the night, something ineffable causes tears to flow and the soul to escape from the body and to coalesce in an embrace.

"One against the other, so close that we are embraced by the same shudder, we magniloquently extoll the May night, then when nothing more remains to be said, we remain silent for a long time and watch the same star, believing that the night is infinite and letting the tears on our cheeks flow together and fuse our souls in an immaterial embrace."[23]

Rising earlier than the others, we would hasten to the woods on sunny days. The forest shimmered with cool dew and the grass sparkled in the sun's rays. In the valley deepened and etherealized by the haze, everything was wondrous. Everything breathed new life and extolled the new day: our souls were lost in reverence.

Stimulated by our intoxication with these things, we longed to see the sunrise—a vain desire since the days were long. I came at daybreak and tapped softly on your door; you were only dozing; you arose and dressed hastily. But the house was still asleep, all the doors were closed, and we were unable to leave.

Then in your room with the window open to the cool dawn, and our bodies slightly chilled even though pressed

---

[23] This passage recalls the Tristan legend as well as earlier and later writings that stress gratification through denial: the Orphic cult and Platonism, the troubadours and the chivalric tradition, Dante, German Romanticism.

closely together, we watched the last stars fade away and the tinged haze appear. Then when its crimson turned to brightness under the sun's first rays, morning songs echoed through our giddy, empty heads and we went back to sleep, intoxicated by our joy.

Tuesday

Multiply emotions. Not just one life in one isolated body; make your soul the host of several bodies. Feel it vibrate to the emotions of others as well as to your own and it will forget its own griefs when it ceases to think only of itself. The outer life is not violent enough; more poignant tremors result from inner surges of rapture. Let it feed on admiration; then it will be haughtier and its vibrations stronger. Not realities but chimeras, for the poet's imagination brings out more clearly the ideal truth hidden behind the appearance of things.[24]

Let the soul never fall back into inactivity; it must be nurtured anew on surges of rapture.

(1887)

Plan of Conduct[25]

Freedom: reason denies it. Even if it did not exist, still we would have to believe in it.

We are shaped by definite influences: we must therefore discern them.

---

[24] The notion of the role of the poet in bringing out the truth hidden behind the appearance of things, though probably suggested by Schopenhauer, was nurtured by the Symbolists. Gide defended the doctrine of the Symbolists in his second work, *Narcissus* (1892).

[25] Pages rediscovered (note by André W.). (Gide's note.)

Let will be dominant everywhere: we should do as we please. We should choose our influences.

Let everything serve to instruct me.

(3 *June,* 1887)

"I wanted to speak of many things, but everything besieges me. I wanted to devote some attention to my *Symbolism* which is now taking shape, but then came the memory of Notre-Dame and the white-robed children's choir seen by lamplight behind the railings of the main altar. The children were all singing and their voices were clear, creating the impression of an angelic choir; a minor cadence, relentlessly repeated and always unexpected, rose to the top of the vault. I also wanted to speak . . . but my thoughts drifted aimlessly, borne along by the melody of a quartet recently heard. I write because poetry overflows my soul and vainly seeks expression through words. Emotions transcend thoughts . . . and yield pure harmony.

". . . Then words, disconnected words, tremulous sentences, something resembling music.

"It is midnight and I am sleepy but unable to sleep, for I am consumed by love. Everything around me sleeps; I am alone and I weep. The air is warm and it is raining outside—a spring rain that make all nature fruitful. And the air played on the cello and remembered during the night assuages my delirium, lulls, soothes, consoles. Thoughts of grief, of madness, of love, of ecstasy are lost in restful sleep. . . .

". . . Submit, my soul; weep and pray for a long while

as sweet night brings intoxication. Weep and submit, my soul. Pray."

(1887)

". . . Or flesh in disguise. Rotten flesh! It appears everywhere in disguise.

"Consider the source of poetry . . . writhings of desire and nerves vibrating to the fascination of colors because of a small quantity of fluid dispersed throughout the body! Oh, what prose, what sordid prose at the bottom of it all!

"But such is responsible for the flower, the supreme poetry of the plant. Here diapered petals unfold themselves beneath erect stamens, like a sumptuous bed of unconscious delights. O poet's unconsciousness! blindness! vain belief in an inspiring Muse! Puberty excites the poet, making him wander about on starry nights under the illusion that he is extolling the ideal . . . until verses elude him. Then the stream of poetry that overwhelms him is converted into orgies in the arms of a courtesan.

"The derivative is indeed sublime! Indeed, it makes man think of himself as God! Beautiful, moonlight nights that evoke pure poetry (Musset) . . . but dogs also bay at the moonbeams!

"What is pure and what sullies cannot be known, for the connection between the two essences is so subtle and their causes so intermingled that a vibration in one is manifested in the other. An abundance of blood makes a generous heart. If Swift had known love, he might have written psalms. . . . And you tell me, friend, that I should not worry about my body but should let it pasture in the fields that it covets. But the flesh corrupts the soul, once it has been corrupted! New wine cannot be put into rotting vessels! The flesh lays claim to the soul unless the soul wins control at the outset. The soul must be the master and not the slave.[26]

"Then I am romantic because my blood pulses within me. . . . Even so, the illusion of the ideal is good and I wish to preserve it."

(Poubazlanec, Sept., 1887)

"Your advice is striking, O Ar***. And so is your theory! 'Free the soul by giving the body what it asks!' you say. And you would hold me in even higher esteem if I did. . . . But friend, the body would have to ask for what is possible; if I gave it what it asks, you would be the first to raise a hue and cry; besides, could I satisfy it?[27]

"Your complacency is also striking! 'The struggle naught availeth,' you said to yourself. 'The soul must not exhaust itself in unworthy conflicts.' Yielding beforehand, you spared yourself the effort. But you must know that gangrene of the flesh infects the soul. No desire of mine fails to reverberate throughout my soul.

"And you set yourself as an example. Certainly, I admire you. Your outlook is broad and you take life as life will probably take me eventually. But what I have not told

---

[26] The allusion to the courtesan probably has no parallel in the life of the author. We learn from his journals, however, that he began at an early age to practice the solitary vice that caused him to be expelled from school, to incur his mother's disapproval, and subsequently perhaps to associate sin with sex.

[27] It is possible that this is the first allusion in any of Gide's writings to his sexual aberrance.

you, what you must never learn lest your serenity be disturbed, is the complete shattering of my dreams when you, obviously disillusioned, told me all this. Oh, I had placed you on a higher plane! And tears on my wounded pride whose futility I suspected for the first time! Disgust bordering on nausea on looking at life, the life that must be lived! I prefer my dream. My dream![28]

"You smiled as you said these things and I smiled as I listened, but I no longer understood your words. One thought alone made tears flood my heart: 'He returned to the girl and was not recognized by her.'

"Not recognized! Lord, is it possible? My heart ached throughout the night. Why this sadness? Such things must be. Why should she have recognized him? She had seen so many afterwards, and features inexorably fade from memory.

"But he had given you everything! Did you know? Had he dared tell you? How depressing is all this, how depressing! Fie! If this is the life that must be lived. . . .

"I prefer my dream, Lord! I prefer my dream."

(*July* 1887)
"I detest their advances, their whispered or subtly intoned words, their ghoulish or siren voices—I detest everything about them.

---

[28] From earliest childhood the author evidenced a vivid imagination and a preference for dreams in contrast to reality. His answer to a question put to him in his old age might be cited to support theories he first formulated on the basis of Schopenhauer's *The World As Will and Idea*. When asked whether Madeleine was the model for Alissa, he replied, "She *became* Alissa."

"And when I walk down the street, I leave the sidewalks and quickly take to the pavement. From a distance I see them turning, pacing back and forth . . . and their gestures, their supposed designs forever intrigue me. I would like to find out. . . .

"It was two years ago and it was for the first time. As a matter of fact it was the only time, for now I am careful and walk at a distance from them. One was singing a sad refrain; a little mockingly but tenderly, and with such a thin, weak voice. . . . As I passed near her she turned around and made a sign, without stopping her singing.

"It was the first time, one of the first nights of spring. The air was warm and the melody nerve-racking. . . . Tears filled my eyes. I could not help turning and running away. She laughed shrilly and another one who was loitering nearby called out: 'There is nothing for you to be afraid of, pretty boy.' The emotion was so violent that I thought I would faint; blood rushed to my face; I blushed from shame, from shame for them; I felt that I had been sullied by the mere fact that I had heard their words. My temple throbbed, my eyes were dimmed by a flood of tears. I ran away.

"But I shall remember the singing shadow beneath the blooming chestnuts, the flickering gaslight and the warm, distracting spring night; then the burst of laughter, as sharp as a broken object; and the tears that I shed. Yes, I shall always remember. The episode was unusually poetic.

"I am writing these things this evening because the season is the same, because the air is just as warm and because everything helps me to remember. I had played the scherzo by Chopin that I still remember and, afterwards I ran through the countryside, intoxicated by sonorities, harmonies. The sky had no moon but was bright with stars; although there were no clouds, rain began to fall, warm rain almost like dew.

"And the air was filled with the perfume of moist summer dust."[29]

Friday

I kept thinking about it until it became an obsession. Last night I dreamed that I was following a path lined by shadows and that on both sides of me writhed naked couples. I could not see their bodies but sensed their embraces. I was overcome by dizziness and, to avoid stumbling, was walking in the middle of the road, alone and erect, with my eyes raised to keep from seeing anything and my hands raised above my head. In the sky shone a few stars. I heard their love-making in the shadows.

I read in the Book of Revelation words containing mysterious promises:

Thou hast a few names which have not defiled their garments; and they shall walk with me in white; for they are worthy.

He that overcometh, the same shall be clothed in white raiment.

To him that overcometh will I give of the hidden

---

[29] Noteworthy here is the characteristic link between sex and sin, attraction and repulsion with respect to the same object, and the practice of employing external surroundings as memory aids.

manna—a white stone on which no man knoweth saving he that receiveth it.
Then I meditated and made virtuous resolutions."[30]

My dreams were splendid. I wrote:

(*March* 1886)
"I would like at twenty-one, the age when passion bursts forth, to subdue it through frenzied, intoxicating toil. I would like, while others pursue vain pleasures, merrymaking and debauchery, to taste the sequestered delights of the monastic life. Alone, absolutely alone, or perhaps surrounded by a few white-robed Carthusians, by a few ascetics; sequestered in some rustic Carthusian monastery in the open countryside, in a sublime and stern setting. I would like to have a bare cell and to lie upon the floor with a horsehair pillow under my head; nearby, a huge but plain praying stool; in the alcove, the Bible always open; overhead, a lamp always lighted. I would like during periods of sleeplessness to experience violent raptures in the terrifying darkness that envelops me as I become totally engrossed in the study of a verse. No noise except perhaps the occasional heavy rumblings of mountains, the dismal voices of glaciers or the midnight psalms chanted on a single note by the Carthusians who keep watch.

"I would like to live fully with only time to pursue me: to eat when hungry, to sleep whenever I chose once my

---

[30] His *Journals* reveal that Gide's virtuous resolutions were made repeatedly only to be broken whenever his demons overpowered him. The *Notebooks* represent his first attempt to escape through his art from the clutches of his demons.

task had been completed. I would wear the white mantle, scapulary and sandals. In my cell I would have a huge oak table and on it, wide open, a few books; a big lectern for working while standing up; rows of books above the bed. I would read the Bible, the Vedas, Dante, Spinoza, Rabelais, the Stoics; I would learn Greek, Hebrew, Italian; and my mind would take pride in its vitality. There would be orgies of learning, and the mind would emerge stupefied, broken, as did Jacob after his struggle with the Angel —and, like him, the victor. And when exasperated flesh rebelled and erupted in a rash of desires, pain caused by the lash of discipline would soon quell the body! Or a frantic race through the mountain, past cliffs and as far as the snow, until panting flesh cried out for relief, exhausted, vanquished . . . or a plunge into deep snow— and an extraordinary shiver resulting from the icy contact."[31]

As a very young child I was ignorant of some things to which I had been exposed.

"Later on," I thought, "I will not have mistresses. All my loves will tend toward harmony."

I dreamed of nights of love in the presence of the organ. The melody was an almost palpable fiction, like a nebulous Beatrice, *fior gittando sopra e d'interno,* like a chosen Lady, immaterially pure, with the deep blue folds of her trailing sapphire-studded gown shimmering in the pale light and

---

[31] Parts of the *Notebooks* were written while the author was in seclusion near the Grande Chartreuse. He viewed the monastery, considered visiting it as a tourist, decided against the visit.

slowly assuming musical patterns. I hoped that she would receive all my tenderness. I was a child and thought only of the soul; I was already living in a dream world; my soul was freeing itself from my body; and my dream of better things was exquisite. Later I separated them so completely that I am no longer the master; each goes its own way, the soul dreaming of ever more chaste caresses and the body carelessly adrift.

Wisdom would dictate that they be kept in check, that their paths be made to converge, and that the soul not seek distant loves in which the body cannot share.

"They do not complain; they make accusations. They do not explain; they condemn. What they will never understand is the struggle to BELIEVE, waged against impossible odds so long as the slightest degree of reason protests. They think that the will to believe is enough! And the most astounding part is that they think they can believe through reason. What especially outrages me is mock religion; bigotry and pretended mysticism sometimes make me doubt that there is a true religion. Bigots are not aware of the harm that their example can do to those who truly seek after the true God; they are not aware that in their complacency they are often themselves an object of scandal. . . ."[32]

(*Midnight, 30 December, 1887*)
"Shall I write? . . . What?

---
[32] Gide seems here to anticipate his own paradoxical development, which prevented the consummation of his marriage even while permitting him to father an illegitimate daughter.

"I am happy.

"I am afraid of forgetting.

"I would like for the memory of my happiness to endure beyond time.

"If only it were possible in the boredom of the tomb to relive life incessantly and to feel gently, as in a dream at night, bitterness and joy—but from such a distance as to cause no more suffering than the memory of griefs.

"I am afraid of forgetting.

"On these pages I wish to preserve—as one preserves dried flowers to recall dissipated perfumes—I wish to preserve the memories of my fleeting youth in order that I may recall it later.

"Today I spoke with her. I told her my radiant dreams and my high hopes. Today I understood that she loved me still. I am happy! . . . What shall I write?

"I write because I am afraid of forgetting.

"And now all of that is only in my memory. . . .

"But perhaps the memory of old things still subsists beyond the tomb."

It was in a wretched room. Poor people were weeping over their dead child (7 February, 1887). I had come without saying anything, for I did not want her to find out until later. I brought them some money; I wished that I could comfort them. I forced myself to speak to them but was embarrassed by my exalted ideas; my sadness on seeing them was certainly sincere, but I experienced it in such a different way; I do not know how to humble myself. I dared not speak to them about heaven since my own belief was too weak; I was uncertain and ill at ease even though my heart was overflowing.

Now I saw the door opening. Emmanuèle entered.

"Is it you, Emmanuèle?"

She passed in front of me with no show of emotion, as if she did not see me. She stood next to the bed where the child lay. She looked at its pale face and I saw her eyes fill with tears. I drew near her and tried to grasp her hand with mine.

"No," she said, pushing me away.

Then kneeling, she prayed aloud. Retreating to the shadows, I heard her sad prayer and felt humble. Then she departed, and I went with her. While walking along, I kept hoping that she would say something about our meeting, but she was too overcome by emotion to comment on it. Her words were meant to explain her sudden departure, or perhaps to break the embarrassing silence.

"Let us leave them," she said. "It is good for them to grieve. Let us not console them now. Our words would not be sincere. Their hope will be renewed by their tears. We must come back, for a kindness can not be left undone once the first step has been taken; it is an obligation that must be fully discharged."

But no sooner had we returned than she put her forehead against my cheek.

"My brother," she whispered.

Her emotion was now too much for her. As she raised her eyes I saw that they were filled with tears. Compassion sapped my strength, but her confession of utter helplessness compelled me to be strong.[33]

I asked her—diffidently, since both of us were overly modest about such things—I asked her to return to the place with me. There she was sweet, patient, sincere—and paid no attention to me; I was attentive only to her and did my utmost to elicit a compensatory smile. . . . But the end soon came.

"Watch out!" she once told me, "Your concern is for me, not them."

Once again I was separated from her.

Providence: their life in its entirety is based on a hypothesis; if they were shown their mistake, they would no longer be able to justify their existence. But who would show them? They will never know whether or not they were mistaken in their belief. If there is nothing, they will never know the difference. Meanwhile, they believe; they are happy or find consolation in their hope. The doubting soul is torn asunder.[34]

"Philosophize? What arrogance! Philosophize with what? with reason? Who guarantees us the soundness of our reason? what is the source of the authority which we

---

[33] Frequently in Gide's writings we find an allusion to his concern for Madeleine, dating back presumably to his discovery of her mother's infidelity and his intense longing at that time to protect her against the harshness of a counterfeit world.

[34] These same notions form the substructure of *The Immoralist* (1902).

accord it? Our only assurance would be in thinking that it is a gift of a providential God—but reason denies God.

"If we argue that reason came about by a slow transformation, by a gradual adaptation to phenomena, we may well discuss the phenomena—but beyond that?

"And even if we grant that it comes from God, there is still nothing to guarantee us of its infallibility.

"We can only hazard opinions. An affirmation is open to criticism, for it is arbitrary and destructive.

"Narrow minds which think that theirs is the only truth! Truth is multiple, infinite, as diverse as there are minds to think—and no truths are challenged except by the mind of man."

Everyone is right. Things BECOME true as soon as someone believes in them. Reality is within us; our mind creates its Truths. And the best truth will not be the one sanctioned by reason. "Men are guided by emotions and not by ideas."[35] "The tree is known by its fruit," and a doctrine by what it suggests.

"The best doctrine is the one which through its message of love will persuade man to worship joyfully; which will comfort in times of distress by offering a vision of happiness promised to those who mourn; which will call grief an ordeal and enable the soul to hope in spite of everything. The best doctrine is the one which offers the greatest consolation. *Lord! To whom would we go? Thou hast the words of eternal life!*

---
[35] Ribot.

"Reason will ridicule but, in spite of all philosophical objections, the heart will always need to believe."[36]

"ΣΥΜΠΑΘΕΙΝ—to suffer together, to vibrate together. Imagination is all powerful, even in matters of the heart. Charity depends on our ability to imagine the griefs of others and make them our own. Thus is the life of the soul multiplied. And thus does compassion assuage grief.

"A heart vibrating to the emotions of all men, throughout time and space, and doing so voluntarily though spontaneously: that is what we need."

We used to read aloud on autumn evenings when they had assembled between the hearth and the lamp. Thus we read Hoffmann and Turgenev.

Everyone listened, but the modulations in my voice were for you alone. I read to you over their heads.

We studied German together, though we already knew the language. The lessons were a pretext for leaning over the same book and being excited by the discovery of subtleties of meaning as we translated passages.

That is how we became acquainted with *Die Braut von Messian*, *Die Heimkehr*, and *Die Nordsee*.

German has whispered alliterations which make it a better medium than French for expressing vague yearnings.

---

[36] The conflicts between faith and reason, appearance and reality, carnal passion and ideal love are familiar antinomies that motivate much of Gide's art.

One evening it was raining and those who had gathered there had been talking for a long time.

"André," said V***, "will you read a little?"

I began the *Expiation,* which she did not know. It is indeed a soothing work. Reading the words with subtle inflections, I made the violent emotions that were flooding my soul flow into yours. ΣΥΜΠΑΘΕΙΝ: to experience together violent emotions.[37]

I did not see you. You were sitting in the shadow, but I felt your look when I read:

And their soul sang in the brass bugle.

The sun was setting. Evening shadows were invading the room. No longer able to see clearly enough to read, I closed the book and recited:

Not one retreated. Sleep, heroic dead! . . .

When the lamp was brought in for us, it seemed to awaken us from a dream. . . .

"Listen," I said to you. "Pay close attention to what I am saying."

I wanted to go over a difficult problem concerning German metaphysics that had bothered me for a long time. I saw that the attempt to follow my reasoning was causing wrinkles to mar your brow, but the obstacles that I had already cleared goaded me onward, and I continued to speak. I would have liked for our minds to travel to-

---

[37] The notion that in Madeleine he had found a kindred soul (an Echo for his Narcissus) persisted for years in Gide's imagination despite indications to the contrary on her part.

gether along every byway; I suffered when learning without you; I needed to feel your presence; I thrilled to your emotions more than to my own. But these heights were too lofty; your spirit fluttered helplessly and grew tired.

I suffered much over such things. When you were not there and overpowering emotion forced me to speak, my mother soon tired of my expositions, for she lacked your benevolent patience. When she became listless, I fell silent and my rebuffed soul shivered in its solitude.

I was then a child. I did not understand that the mind is nothing and passes away while the soul still remains after death.

The mind changes, grows feeble, passes away; the soul remains.

"What is the SOUL?" they will ask.

The SOUL is our WILL TO LOVE.

We still said "brother" and "sister," but with a smile. Our hearts were no longer deluded. Yet you wanted to be deluded. You were afraid that we would go too far, and you hoped that you could allay your incipient fears by using a familiar word as a decoy. You thought perhaps that the word would evoke the thing and that if we always called each other brother and sister, our relationship would be fraternal. But in spite of our intentions, alien inflections marked our words; they became more intimate, more endearing, more mystical when whispered to each other. When you said "my brother" and I answered "little sister," our hearts quivered at the involuntary tenderness of our voices.[38]

Long autumn days . . . sitting by the fireside while rain fell outside . . . engrossed in reading for hours at a time . . . and you sometimes came to lean over my shoulder and read.

I was reading *The Golden Ass* when you came, as was your custom, to read over my shoulder.
"This is not for you, little sister," I said as I pushed you away from me.
"Then why are you reading it?"
You smiled somewhat waggishly—and I closed the book.

Playing games during our childhood, seeing landscapes, conversing at length, reading together when we knew nothing and could discover everything together. . . .
All these things mean nothing to others but gradually shaped us and made us so nearly identical. . . .
A stranger, Emmanuèle? . . .
Would a stranger remember the beloved dead?
Oh that he had never known them! Oh that he had never seen their smiles! When you chose to speak of them, he would not understand. Then you would fall silent, aware of your loneliness.

(incomplete)

---

[38] Gide's fraternal relation with his cousin Madeleine probably began at an early age. He was present at her father's funeral in 1890, just as she had been present at the funeral of his father ten years earlier.

I no longer know either where or when: It was in a dream.

One night I was weeping for both of us—and your dear shadow came close to me. I felt your hand on my brow and saw your sweet smile.

But I was still weeping.

"Well, do you want to, André? . . ." you asked without moving your lips. Your smile illuminated my soul.

In my soul I have kept the music of your words, and on my brow the memory of your sweet caress.

28 May

The last three days I have reread your letters. I have kept them all, but they give a poor impression of you. If they were all I had to remember you by, I would think you waggish, rather fickle, always evasive and elusive. Your mind forces your soul to remain aloof.[39]

From time to time, however, it would suddenly cry out to me, and it was then so plaintive—like a prisoner.

"Do not withhold your affection, my brother," you said. "I prefer it above all else."

And later on, after a separation, you said: "I can not accept the idea of life without you."

And there was still more. There were fleeting moments of tenderness, quickly squelched by the mind; then in the next letter, ironically you made fun of yourself and of me for having believed you.

---

[39] Frequently and for many years Madeleine's actions apparently belied Gide's hopes.

The reason was that far from me, your mind was again dominating your soul.

Yes, sometimes your soul managed to break free, and when it spoke, its ardor astounded even me. At times I questioned your tenderness since you refused to acknowledge it to yourself; I thought that I loved you much more.

The last night before we were to part for a long time, I told you these things and wept—as much from emotion as from the wish to be assured by you—for I was comforted by only the most tenuous hope, and when I was uncertain your absence made me fear the worst. But you finally tired of the silence.

"Oh, André," you exclaimed tearfully, "never will you know how much I loved you!"

Your mind is stubborn, despotic. It would have you be domineering. You again resorted to mockery. O the smirk on your lips! I had to obey immediately or you would evade me. Silence until I gave in. You knew that I would always come back to you. That was what made you strong; I was not sure of you; I gave up quickly.

Then came sweet reconciliation. We managed to be together more often, and our souls were all the more loving when we were apart because we had restrained them.

Your mind! I will find fault with it because it irritates me. It is your mind that I know best, and yet it is not similar in any respect to my own. You are afraid to admire without passing judgment. You would like to keep your reason unimpaired; whatever is immoderate terrifies you

—as much as it attracts me. I resent your not having trembled in the face of Luther's grandeur; then I sensed your femininity, and I suffered. You understand things too well and do not love them enough.

But our souls—they are so alike that they can not know each other! . . .[40]

I wrote to Pierre:

But let them believe. What right have you to deprive them of the joys of believing? What will you give them in exchange? They are absolutely right even if they are mistaken. To believe in possession is as comforting as to possess . . . and are not all possessions chimerical? They are duped by a mirage of eternity and uplifted by their hope. If there is nothing after life, who will return to tell them? Nor will they be aware of not existing after death; they will never know that they have not lived on eternally. But nothing must stand in the way of their belief here and now—it is the basis for their happiness.

I remember having shown her those lines.

"O André!" she exclaimed. "If things were the way you say they are, faith would be an illusion. Only truth is worthy of belief, even though it might offer no hope. I prefer to suffer through not believing than to believe in a lie."

---

[40] Madeleine, though frightened and insecure because of her childhood experiences, was older than Gide and had enough common sense to refrain from marrying him until after his mother's death. It is doubtful that the two ever fully understood each other.

are too much for me. I am [...] your faith; I wish it had [...] had cried out in the void! [...]lorn with yours for its com-[...]wn compassion. You might [...]u did not flinch, and now

[...]ding Spinoza—oh, how these [...]iring his divine plan. [...], Emmanuèle—this unortho-[...]e mind," you said. "A book [...]uld know it? [...]ly acquainted and no longer withheld their secrets. ... knew each other's thoughts before speaking and we knew how they would be phrased. I made a game of it. When we were talking I would anticipate the word that was to come from your lips and take it away from you before they parted. But familiarity with the mind did not extend to the soul. . . . One soul pursued the other but was always deluded and led astray by the succession of thoughts that flowed in parallel fashion through our minds. The soul was enchanted by an illusory similitude, one that involved not the soul but a frivolous mind.

It was like the lover in the legend of Ondine. Pursuing her one evening, he imagined that he saw her changing image in the will-o'-the-wisp hovering over a pond. Seduced by the captivating illusion, he dashed after it only to be disillusioned. He wept when the phantom disintegrated between his fingers.

(Our souls were obscured by our thoughts. When one of them darted forth, it would skid along smooth surfaces. The slope formed by our thoughts was so inviting and the succession of our thoughts so effortless that our souls were tempted to go wherever our thoughts coincided.)

We liked to lose ourselves in distant memories. By virtue of associations that transcended time and space and unsuspected relationships, one word was enough to evoke a host of dreams. The word was never bare but it had one and the same legend for both of us; it evoked from the past many emotions, many passages that we had read—both when we had said things and when we had read them. It was never the word itself but the recall of the past. That is why we derived so much pleasure from quoting poets—not because we experienced something through them but because they reminded us of so many things!

Then one word often signified a whole sentence known only to us—it was only a bare word to others. One word was the beginning of a verse or of a thought, another marked the end. For instance, when we were walking around the house one evening, I began:

Listen! my dear . . .

and you understood:

Listen to the night gently descending.[41]

Then it became a task, an obsession. We had always to watch for companion thoughts and to bring them to light even though we recognized them for what they were beforehand. . . . We no longer thought but watched each other think, and with the same result. But we were tormented by the need to test the similitude and would voice our thoughts even though we could have remained silent and communicated without words.

We anticipated sentences, snatching them from each other's lips before they were uttered—and sometimes as we both waited for a thought from the other, the same thought would come to both of us.

On summer evenings it was with Chopin, Baudelaire. . . .

Leisurely dreams the moon tonight . . .
How would I love you, O night, without stars. . . .

But our tired lips left the verse incomplete and we let our eyes give more precise expression to our feelings of tenderness tinged with desire.

Some of those around us were upset by our close relationship, which we never tried to conceal. They tried to separate us, to erect barriers between us; but it was already too late, for we communicated by means of signs unnoticed by others. Instead, they quickened our interest in the mystery of sign languages, and we created our own

---

[41] Pierre Louis praised Gide for his choice of quotations, particularly this one from Baudelaire (and gave rise to the suspicion that he considered the quotations superior to the text).

solitude in their midst. By shackling them, they revealed to us our desires.

"Phenomena are signs that make up a language—the language of the desires that lie behind phenomena. Only desires matter, and they must be understood.
"To understand is nothing, but to be understood—that is the problem and the source of anguish. The soul throbs and would have the other know—but can not and feels isolated. Then come gestures, words, awkward explanations and material symbols for imponderable outbursts of feeling—and the soul despairs.
"Nor is that anything. The worst suffering is that of two souls unable to approach each other. *Thou hast built a wall around me to prevent my going out* (Jeremiah).
"They hug the wall that keeps their courses parallel, and they collide and bruise each other."

"Neither words nor gestures give shape to thought—they proceed from the frivolous mind. But the inflection of an excited voice, the lines on the face, especially the look—these are the eloquence of the soul. Through them the soul finds expression. They must be studied, dominated, made into docile interpreters.
"I study them in front of a looking glass. They would have laughed if they had seen me looking into my own eyes and, by night, becoming almost hypnotized by the changes undergone by dark pupils as I searched for the outward manifestation of emotions through sparkling or sorrowful looks, for the alignment or narrowing of the

eyebrows and the wrinkles on the brow that should accompany words of passion, of elation, of sorrow. . . .

"Comedian? Perhaps. . . . But I play myself, and the roles best played are those best understood."[42]

"Then it becomes painful never to lose sight of myself while searching anxiously for the word, the gesture, especially the look and the inflection of the voice which will best reveal the secret emotions of my soul.

"Often preoccupation over appearing to be excited supplants the genuine emotion. Many times I have been with you, Emmanuèle, and felt the true, spontaneous emotion vanish under the attempt to force it to the surface.

"Suffering consists in being unable to reveal oneself and, when one happens to succeed in doing so, in having nothing more to say."

To understand each other is nothing. What matters is a mating of our souls.

"I need to caress someone. My repressed caresses have not been restricted to one person but lavished on everyone. My caress is an embrace; I tend instinctively to embrace others."

The sad part, and the part that has caused me to suffer acutely, is that the soul can reveal its tenderness only

---

[42] Paul Claudel once rebuked Gide for his fascination with mirrors. Gide completed his first book and simultaneously practiced the art of self-scrutiny by setting down his thoughts as he stood before a secretary equipped with a mirror.

through caresses which are signs of unchaste desires. The soul is mistaken, deluded. . . . And then in me the gesture awakened the thought. . . .

I must remain frigid in order that there be no mistake, even on the part of my soul . . . for sometimes. . . . I must simply clasp and release her hand, bid her goodnight without the kiss of peace. My heart may quiver—but imperceptibly and not violently.

"Loving, adoring, impassioned caresses—I am obsessed by the act of caressing. I would like an all-absorbing, all-encompassing caress, or complete oblivion of self, which constitutes ineffable ecstasy. That is why I suffer so much in the presence of the beauty of statues, for then my being does not blend with theirs but contrasts with it.

*. . . Quoniam nihil inde abradere possunt,
Nec penetrare et abire in corpus corpore toto.*

"A little flesh is still infused by virtue of the transparency of the marble. The desire to possess torments me and I suffer piteously, both physically and spiritually, through awareness of the impossibility of possession. I am corrupted, not intoxicated, by the sight of the *Thorn Puller, Apollo,* the mutilated torso of *Diana Reposing.*

Nec satiare queunt spectando corpora coram.

"And I suffer still when I think that they will never feel my caresses.

> *Superfluous, implacable splendor,*
> *O beauty, what pain you cause me!*
>
> *Impossible union of souls through bodies*
> *... tormented by an embrace.*

"Here is the strange part, and the part that has caused me to suffer so much. The soul blends in with everything else, and it becomes impossible to determine whether it harbors desire or whether the flesh is disguised as reverence. *So insistently is the soul pushed toward the mysterious bed....*

> *A caress comes to an end, is ephemeral,*
> *My soul stirs at the sound of a kiss....*

"*Et non erat qui cognosceret me* . . . Nor the others, for souls can not know each other. The courses followed by those who are most nearly alike are still PARALLEL.

"So you see that I do not desire you. Your body disturbs me and carnal possession frightens me. We do not love each other according to the dictates of rational love. You could never belong to me, for the things that we long for are never possessed."[43]

---

[43] This section seems to recapitulate Gide's adolescence and to anticipate his predicament after he had realized the full consequences of the complete separation of (carnal) pleasure and (ideal) love. His reaction to statues is recorded in his *Journals,* and his sensuousness and sensitivity to physical contact endured a lifetime and caused him alternately to tend toward renunciation and affirmation of the desire "to remain carnal unto death."

12 June

A letter from Pierre and some books. He writes of Paris, of the struggle and of some early triumphs. . . . Farewell to philosophical calm; this gust of feverish air intoxicates me and rouses dormant visions of glory. My ambitions were slumbering in solitude, but now they have been awakened. Everything militates against my secluded life: a flurry of excitement, of preparations back there. I shall arrive too late for everything.[44]

The letter is really good for me. My pride is cut to the quick but I am not defeated. The lash that brings the blood gives me the energy to run even faster. Oh, how strong I feel!

I shall arrive suddenly, without warning, and blow a loud trumpet blast—or perhaps remain unknown but hear my work acclaimed (for I shall withhold my name).[45]

I must work frantically, *dishonestly*. I shall leave here only after the work is finished. And to avoid further disturbances, I am having my mail sent to an imaginary place.

His writing is perfect—callously, impeccably, inexor-

---

[44] Gide was convinced that he had something to say to his generation, that his problem of formulating an austere ideal to free him from temptations of the flesh and protect him from anguish was a familiar problem, and that his time was limited. Though he had long nurtured the project, he was not able to begin writing systematically until the spring of 1890, when he, aged twenty, broke away from his mother for the first time and secluded himself at Menthon, near Grenoble. He felt that before the age of twenty-one he had to finish the work—and he did.

[45] Pierre Louis achieved fame (as Pierre Louÿs) before Gide and knew him during the period of the writing of the *Notebooks* but not during the year assigned to it in the *White Notebook*.

ably so. This discourages me, for to me my language was still fluid and boundless. I wanted to give it rhythmic contours—but emotion always made the sentence explode, and I set down only the debris.

The books are by Verlaine, and I did not know him!

This evening, even though the hour was late, I trimmed and stacked the paper that Pierre sent with the books. The sight of white paper intoxicates me. The black signs which I may use to cover them, which will reveal my thoughts and which when reread later will recall today's emotions.

I could not sleep because my simmering thoughts were so uncontrollable. I felt the pressure of latent creative forces. Inspiration became something tangible, and the vision of my work was as dazzling as if the work had already been completed. What splendors of aureoles, what flashes of dawn! Then my burning brow, my grandeur stunned me—disorganized thoughts—the feeling of stumbling, a fall—something on the verge of breaking. . . . Oh, loss of sanity! Suddenly, piously, gripped by indescribable terror, I made a supreme effort to protect my mind and my vision against sudden destruction.

"Forgive me, Lord," I prayed. "I am but a child, a small child lost on a treacherous byway. O Lord, keep me safe and sane!"[46]

---

[46] In the *Black Notebook* (the Manichean twin of the *White Notebook*) we learn that he does lose his mind but not before entrusting his notebooks to a friend for possible publication.

Let style and mood blend. And since this is not plastic art, let music exert its influence. Why not even a strophe?

Put your hand in mine, and let our fingers join,
Put your chin on my shoulder, and let our hearts beat as one,
Let your brow come to rest and let your eyes merge with mine.
But let us stop short of a kiss, for fear that love will intervene.

Let us not speak but listen to the singing of your soul
And to the reply of mine through fingers joined;
Hearts in close communion, looks that reciprocate . . .
Silence—let us not speak.

* * *

Your soul sings in your dark eyes.
Come closer to me, my friend,
You are always too far away.

Closer, ah! come closer still—
How upsetting are your glances!
They seem to smile and your soul to cry.

How far behind your pupils is your soul.

Into the damp darkness of your eyes
Plunges my desire-drenched soul
But your soul keeps retreating
Behind the darkness in your eyes.

> *"Dearly beloved, ah! turn away, ah! turn away from me
> Your eyes, for they disturb me."*
>
> *(Alternate: Schumann)*

Do not look at me. Speak to me instead—I am listening.

> *Oh! speak and I shall see you in my dream
> Not unlike the inflection of your sweet voice.
> Words are unimportant—speak incoherently,
> Speak slowly, think of the harmony
> That your soul will reveal to me.*

* * *

I would like to be lulled to sleep by your words.

* * *

Sometimes I think that pursuit of the elusive soul is a deception and that the soul is but a more subtle manifestation of the mind; reason then advises me to rejoice. Priceless subtleties then ensue:

> *The effort that my soul makes to reach yours must be instinctive, spontaneous. It must be unconscious and the soul must be lost . . . in self-contemplation.*

Still other subtleties.

> *They will not indulge in calling and in contemplating each other. If they escape from the body and leap toward each other in a mutual outburst of desire, they collide or their paths cross, but there is no place for them to come to rest.*

The result is that they meet in mutual admiration and intermingle on the thing admired. They will thus be oblivious to themselves and will not be troubled by enticing looks, and will not exhaust themselves in the attempt to call each other.

For example, I have at times experienced their fusion when we were reading and admiring each other—when both of us prayed for each other in the mourning room with Lucie, when we watched the same star on a flowery May night and let our tears run together as our cheeks touched and we surrendered our souls to each other.

Still other subtleties—traps set by the bantering mind.

"Our communion is still not perfect.

"I sense the confusion in our souls; I do not sense their fusion.

"In order for mine to blend with yours, I must lose the notion of its resistant life, its consciousness of itself. Then the soul becomes passive.

"Thus Nirvana is experienced only as the taste of nothingness in non-life itself. It is negation.

"Our communion will never be perfect; or, if perfect, it will never be experienced as such."

But harmony—music! Music carries the undulation of one soul all the way to the other soul.

Bodies hindered me; they hid the souls. *The flesh is useless.* An embrace should be immaterial.

Possession. An alternative for Allain—and for me. If only I could be convinced. . . .[47]

At night when the body surrenders to sleep, the soul escapes. It flies hurriedly toward distant loves and possesses them immaterially. The body dreams.

Morning comes and the body stirs, awakens, rises. Again it takes possession of the little soul, which is again imprisoned. Distant memories are cause for regret—dear loves recalled merely as dreams . . . for normally you are accompanied by the body, little soul! People do not imagine caresses in the absence of bodies. Ah! If they knew! But they are all blind!

And each evening my soul flies to your side, to the side of the one loved by my soul. Like a weightless bird my soul alights on your lips, and with a slight tremor your lips begin to smile.

With a passionate (*sehnsuchtsvoll*) shout my soul summons yours. Like two merging flames our two souls fuse and plunge more deeply into space filled with harmonies produced by the beating of their wings.

They have taken their flight through space. It is night and the moon is beautiful. From vast sleeping forests rise masses of fog. Together we fly toward sweeter heavens, toward warmer breezes whose caresses our souls desired.

Through pines where the wind sings—in the forest

---

[47] The enigmatic conclusion may express doubt—conscious or unconscious—on the part of the author. In this section and others we find parallels to Manicheism, based on the doctrine of the two contending principles of good (spirit) and evil (the body).

chilled by sparkling dewdrops that fall on us as tears from sagging branches—over wheat that extends beyond the range of sight on the empty horizon and inclines at our passage, like a billowing sea traversed by gusts—to moist slopes where the petals of dormant flowers, finally refreshed, perfume the stars with their ecstatic dreams.

Through the night's silence our souls pursue their swift untroubled flight.

Death when it comes will not separate our souls.
Beyond the tomb they will take flight and again join.
For separation of bodies does not make soul solitary.
The world can only separate bodies.
Nothing can stand in the way of the loving soul, for love has conquered all.
Love is stronger than death.

"Reason!" they say, and to me this is sheer arrogance. What has their Reason done?

It is always contrasted with the soul; when the heart acts, reason interferes.

It is repulsed by devotion. The sublime is always ridiculous. Daring, poetry—everything that makes life worth living is foolish. Reason would protect us; it is utilitarian, but it makes life intolerable to the soul.

It is despised by true lovers, for one who loves no longer lives for himself. His life is but a means of loving. If he finds one which is better and which will make for closer union, he will neglect—perhaps reject, forget—his own life in favor of it.

I have never had any happiness which reason sanctions.

(*August* 1888)

"It was already late and the others, tired, sat down to wait for us.

"The other hillside, ascended with great difficulty, sloped gently downward. The sun bathed the plain in golden, peaceful rays. At a bend in the stream was a castle with a slate roof; around it were the lower roofs of white farmhouses; under a thick fog was the pink heath and, protruding above it, a crest of grey rocks.

"The foliage of two chestnuts blended above our heads. On the slopes of the meadow, women were stacking hay; amorous sounds filled the air; and hovering over and enveloping everything was a radiant serenity, a penetrating tenderness that seemed to emanate from things and rise with the odor of the hay when night came. Our souls were refreshed by the setting.

"'Lord,' I exclaimed, *'it is fitting that we remain here! Would you like to? Let us pitch our tent!'*

"Then you smiled, but your smile was so sad that I sensed in it your desolate soul. My own shuddered for an instant. You understood too much and, quickly turning away in your fright, you sadly broke the spell.

"'Come,' you said. 'They are waiting for us. We must leave all this. . . .'"

Emmanuèle and I begged her to sing. We were alone.

* * *

V*** sat down at the piano and began to play and sing Schumann's *The Sorceress*. Her voice was but a puff of air, a fragile vase of emotion—it was pure emotion, with nothing to contain it as it escaped ethereally, revealing her soul. It seemed that the soul itself was singing and replacing her voice.

When she came to the high-pitched notes in the bewitching line *"Es ist shon spät; es ist schon kalt,"* she trembled and quivered like a broken object.

Your emotion was too much for you; tears poured from your eyes; then, ashamed of your confusion and worried because your heart also quivered involuntarily, you darted away. I followed you to your room.

"Oh, leave me!" you said. "Please leave me!"

I went away. I wandered until evening through the fields, my mind undulating with the flood of exaltations produced by remembered harmonies.

Let my soul sense its vitality through the effort to win in its arduous struggle. Then will come dreams of the impossible, of chastity, of faith. Then, endowed with new strength, it will be brave enough to overpower your soul in spite of your belligerent mind.

Your mind! I once resented your mind, your poor mind which was frightened by your troubled soul and which did its utmost to calm your outbursts of feeling. What struggles! And always to resist yourself! You wanted your will to prevail and you set it against invading tenderness.

"I shall never allow myself to be dominated by anything!" you thought.

I misunderstood all that. I only understood that your

mind deprived me of your soul and that your soul desired me.

I sometimes hear your soul cry out softly, but your dominating mind subdues it. One day I shall force it to cry out and prevent your mind from stifling its pleas.

One day I shall force your poor soul to speak. . . .

Music, music—in anguished harmonies your astonished soul will recognize its counterpart and release the tears that it has long restrained. But when I start to play, you become alarmed and flee.

* * *

One summer night—a hot stormy night following a splendid day—all was still without. There was no breeze. My soul was expectant.

You came out on the terrace while the others remained inside. When I saw that you could not flee, I opened the window wide and sat down at the piano. The sounds came to you in waves.

I began to play Chopin's first *Scherzo*—brutally, noisily, almost as a prelude at first, for I did not wish to startle your soul. When I came to the *più lento*, I muted the melody and it cried, morbidly sweet. As pearls drop from a fountain, the high notes fell, obstinately the same but severally eloquent, while the harmony changed.

I went back to the *agitato* but with all the passion in my heart, making the anguished dissonances quiver. I stopped abruptly before you could break the spell. And I approached you and found you trembling; there were no tears and your eyes were radiant.

"André, why were you playing that?" you asked, and

your voice was so different that I was frightened and dared not answer.

We remained silent.

"Look into the darkness," you finally said, as if alarmed. "Is it not supernatural?"

Lightning flickered noiselessly on the horizon. The air was perfumed with pollen from lime-trees, with the scent of flowering acacias. I tried to take your hand; it was feverous but you rebuffed me.

We remained silent.

"Oh, André," you again interposed, but in a whisper and with your head lowered, "you acted cowardly this evening."

Raindrops were beginning to fall. We went back inside.

The storm broke during the night. You were suffering: feverish and almost delirious.

The next day you stayed in bed and refused to see me.

"My affliction is not serious," you said.[48]

(Thursday)

"My thoughts kept me awake almost all night long. I could not sleep. 'Oh, André, you acted cowardly this evening.' Suddenly I felt you next to me, so frail, so fragile —as if penitent."

"It was wrong for me to do what I did: to upset you,

---

[48] Soon after his arrival at Menthon, where he was writing the *Notebooks,* Gide installed a piano. Though he was an accomplished pianist, he is said to have played his best when no one was in the room and when he suspected that someone outside was listening.

to wish to disturb your soul. . . . And could I satisfy it after altering it?"

"*You acted cowardly!*
"Her contempt! Do not hold me in contempt! . . . What now?"

(*October 5*)
"All day long I experienced infinite sadness amid grey surroundings.
"I collected one by one my sullied hopes, and I cried over each of them.
"All my strength had left me! I no longer dared even desire you from afar."

"I ceased to pursue your soul.
"I shall wait. I shall be there. I shall still be the same. If you have the slightest desire for me, I shall rush to your side—but not until you call me. I shall wait."

(*Sunday*)
"Today I lived close to her but our eyes did not seek each other. I did not draw near you. I was lost in thought almost all day long.
"Waiting.
"We shall travel PARALLEL. That used to drive me to despair."
"I have again started to read my Bible. I must once again ascend the slope which I descended unsuspectingly.
"Oh, how difficult it is!"

I skip over pages—the transition will be too abrupt, but I am tired of recounting everything.

I would like new things—and I see some that are so radiant. . . .

I was sad then. . . . How distant is this "then!" Outside spring is in the air—and I would like to sing:

For the day is approaching, the dawn draws near.

(*October* 18)

"Self-esteem, contentment in the soul! The splendor of virtue, which I at first sought for you, gradually dazzles and attracts me.

"There are loftier emotions, nobler yearnings, more sublime raptures.

"The soul evolves."

(*October* 22)

"For me alone! For me alone!

"They will not understand—what does it matter to me?

"My heart is flooded. I must sing.

"A little harmony rather than words—no sentences—O for words that they might understand!

"*My heart teems with incantations*. My soul floats on a moving tide of modulations and broken arpeggios which rise like a troubled flight of furtive wings and incessantly fall without being resolved.

"Passion flows rhythmically, metrically, quietly . . . passion subsides; the soul meditates."

"ALLAIN.

"In order not to taint her purity, I shall abstain from caressing her—in order not to disturb her soul—and even from the most chaste caresses, from clasping her hand . . . for fear that she may later desire all the more that which I could never give her. And I shall not look into her eyes for fear that she may wish me to come closer and cause me in spite of everything to go so far as to kiss her.

"In this way our souls will remain fearful even though one calls out to the other. . . ."[49]

(October 25)

The soul meditates:

No virtue without effort. My chastity is not virtuous. I love to love because it is sweet for me to love and because I would be loved as much as I love . . . but there is no effort.

Nor does effort count if motivated by the desire for the esteem of another—for her esteem. The effort must be made without hope for reward.

I am searching for the source of virtue.

Virtue would consist in doing good without her knowing about it . . . yes, without my laying claim later to a larger measure of her esteem. . . .

Without her knowing . . . and willfully—is this possible? First, before acting, I would have to promise not to say anything to her—about the act, nor to anyone who would

---

[49] Highly significant in that it anticipates Gide's conduct toward his wife after their marriage, this passage suggests both her role as the mother-sister image and the presentiment of his inability to consummate a physical union with Madeleine, "the only woman he ever loved."

repeat my words to her—to bury the act in my heart. It is at this point that the idea of God is necessary. I would have to appear to myself to be offering it to her like a secret sacrifice whose smoke would rise to her without being seen by men—to promise myself to hide it forever! . . .

But this thought tantalizes me: "What would be the use then—since she would not know about it?"

Mercenary! The reward for good must be found in the good itself; we must not expect it to come from men.

Or take the reward of meriting her esteem—of feeling that when I approach her, I am worthy (a little more worthy at least). Oh, without my saying a word, she would read it in my eyes, would look past my eyes into my soul. . . .

"Never mind," she would say. "I know without being told."

Here again, her esteem would be involved. To be sure, I would have advanced, but not far enough. What else?

I would have to be vilified by her until my rebellious pride crumbles; to accept the unjust accusation without trying to defend myself in order that she might think me worse than I am. That would be struggling, heart-break, triumph!

But suppose that as a result she loved me less?

Well, now! that is the acid test. Virtue consists in feeling that I am above her esteem, that I am more worthy than she thinks. That she would love me less matters not, for I would love her all the more; this would be my reward. I would not be deluded, for I would know that my actions were motivated by the need for self-esteem, by pride; still, I would accept the inevitable, loyally, simply, without pretending to wage gratuitous moral battles with myself.

Yes, that is how things stand. Virtue consists in suffering the loss of her esteem. I must lose her esteem—but how? A lie through which I discredit myself? No, the act itself must be thoroughly pure. The best way is for me to let things drift along, simply, ordinarily; this will cause me to suffer the most, for I am afraid of being encouraged by the test itself, by some slight theatrical element which I might introduce into it.

Then, simply, ordinarily, I shall let myself be discredited by things, by all those things that surround me, by the infinite number of petty, accidental accusations that will cause my aggravated pride to bristle; but I shall restrain it and in the evening, very calm and very lonely, I shall pray and shall slowly kill my mutilated ego.

And I shall love you still more, bless you still more, my sister, because I shall whisper to myself (but not to you) that it is to you that I must become better.

I must deserve you by leaving you—(oh! artless).

"The more abundantly I love you, the less I am loved." (II Cor. 12:15).[50]

"For me alone! For me alone!

---

[50] Alissa, André Walter's feminine counterpart in *Strait Is the Gate*, also practices humility and self-denial in pursuit of Christian glory; as in the case of all other Gidean heroines, she succeeds. She dies and Jerome finally possesses her, recalling again the Tristan legend and the tradition of fulfillment through denial.

"They will not understand . . . but what does it matter?

"I shall always recognize you, dear tears of love, under the mystery (to others) of these sobs, these pleas, these laments. . . .

"Tears? Why tears?"

"I am happy, however . . . she loves me . . . but my soul trembles when night falls.

"In the street they laughed in passing. I did not know who was singing, but the voice was too loud. Then evening came and stillness reigned. The water reflected the pink sky, except under dark bridges.

"And I did not know—I walked like a fool. My head was filled with songs.

"Then evening came and stillness reigned . . . shadows lengthened—and pale night appeared in the pale sky . . . great encompassing night.

"Tears? Why tears. Tears of love, of ecstasy!

"I weep because the night is beautiful and hope floods my soul."

(Midnight, Antibes, Nov. 5)

"It is night. I can not sleep. What are you doing, Emmanuèle? I know that you lie awake. On the balcony the light from your room silhouettes the flowers embroidered on your curtains. What are you doing? It is late. The others are asleep.

"And what was wrong with you this evening? You seemed pensive—pensive over what, my sister? Oh, if only I dared read your soul! . . . Emmanuèle, could it be true? . . . But I am afraid to find out—I wait for you still."

*Oh! I beseech you, daughters of Jerusalem,
Do not awaken, do not awaken my love—
Until she wills it.*

* * *

I sat down at the piano. I had not dared to play for you again since the other evening . . . fearing the worst, doubting. I played at random Schumann's *Novelettes*. You were on the balcony. It was still warm in spite of advancing night. I played at random—and then—you came to listen to me. I had not seen you approach but suddenly the delicate rustling of your dress made me aware of your presence. I trembled so from surprise and confusion that I could no longer play.

"Look!" I said, "You upset me so much when you come up like this . . . I am trembling."

"Why, André? Why?" you asked with a smile.

You did not go away. You remained nearby—and you watched me. I felt your look without seeing it.

Turn your eyes away from me, for they disturb me.

You remained so pensive. Pensive over what, Emmanuèle?

What are you doing now that it is so late? The hour for sleep has come.

Then—a little later on—we were all sitting around the lamp. You had risen to look for a book and then, before you sat down again, you came near me and I felt your delicate hand gently caress my forehead.

I looked at you; bending over me, tenderly, you were smiling, but sadly, pensively. . . . Pensive over what, Emmanuèle?

What are you doing now, so late at night?

Perhaps your soul is also waiting and you are praying.

(*November* 6)

"For the first time I saw your look in a dream.

"You were smiling, but mockingly. I put my hand over my eyes to avoid seeing your look, but I could still see it through my hand."

"You told me at the kiss of dawn: 'I prayed for both of us last night, André.'

" 'Do you think that I did not know, little sister?' I replied.

"Then you looked disturbed; you wanted to speak but fell silent. What did you wish to say?"

(*November* 26)

They are watching us, I know. Especially my mother. She dares not believe; she does not know—and is afraid to find out. She is especially disconcerted by the fact that for the past several days, for reasons incomprehensible to her, I have avoided you. But yesterday when you came up to the piano, I could not help noticing her uneasiness.

Then I had a dream last night, a strange, sweet dream. We were sitting by the lamp in the evening—talking, reading as on other evenings—but I sensed on all sides their mute spying on our movements, as one senses things intuitively in dreams.

Fearfully I observed my actions. Frightened by the notion that you might approach me, I had sat down far away from you.

You, absent-minded, apparently unaware of their looks, came up to me: I was unable to run away, and your hand sought mine as it tried in vain to escape and slowly, tenderly, caressed it.

Around us their faces became animated, their heads nodded, their smiles appeared.

"Aha!" they said, "we knew it all along, all along!"

Their derisive laughter seemed forced. You kept your eyes lowered and continued obstinately to caress my hand, which I tried in vain to withhold.

And that was so strangely sweet that I awoke, as from a nightmare.[51]

Here end the written pages.

My mother was sick. We stood by her bedside and comforted her. I cooled her brow and you gave her water. Both of us were engrossed in a common prayer; all else was forgotten. Our souls, void of everything except pity, void of desire other than that of serving, united in the face of approaching death, not in profane joy, not even startled by the ecstatic embrace long anticipated and

---

[51] This entry strongly suggests that Gide blamed his mother for interfering with his plan to marry Madeleine and extricated himself from the painful situation by idealizing his love for both. Blinded by his own emotions, he was unable to appreciate the soundness of his mother's advice to her niece or the perceptiveness of the latter in rejecting his proposal.

finally realized—and almost without seeing each other because of the dazzling light of virtue which we contemplated and toward which our souls aspired.

All else was forgotten, so lofty were our thoughts.

In the evening you put your hand in mine to pray; then you forgot and removed it as you watched my dear moribund mother fall into peaceful sleep. We remained beside her for a long time.

Both of us kept watch that night in the room where the dying woman slept. Though near, we did not see each other. That was the supreme moment; our souls evolved. Without speaking, as if in a trance, we thought—what thoughts!

Virtue, which first I had sought for you, now dazzled me and exerted on me its pull. . . .

The boundaries of reality were blotted out; I was living a dream.

The next day my mother spoke to me. I have already repeated her words . . . but the sacrifice had already been made in my heart. . . .

Then my mother set their engagement. I know that I saw both of them, Emmanuèle and T***, at the foot of the bed, their hands clasped, and that my mother was giving them her benediction. But all the rest is forgotten —my overwhelming grief seemed unreal and I thought that I was dreaming—there was no longer even a trace of bitterness in my grief.

And what remains now is joy. . . .

(*June* 28)

Some evening I shall recall the past and repeat my words of mourning. . . . Today, however, the sky is too bright, too many birds are singing. I am inebriated by spring and my mind is filled with new lyrics in which our name delicately rimes and alliterates with the names of flowers. It is a sweet melody: an air played on a flute—almost like the warbling of birds—and the sound of wings beneath leaves in visible shadows—O flutes, soaring oboes! . . .

Love transcends mourning and death.
And the alleluias of victory will drown out the song of the willows.
Bless you, beloved mother! Above your bed of suffering our souls found each other again.
You could separate only our bodies, enabling all three of us to find comfort in the serenity of studied virtue; but through a higher, inscrutable will stern virtue, which seemed at first to separate us, became glorious and consummated the chaste desire in our souls.
It is through obedience that I have found her again— in spite of ourselves and because it had to be that way.
Then I departed.
As soon as the period of mourning had ended, they celebrated their marriage . . . their marriage . . . ?
And I departed.
I departed, and took refuge in this solitude, for I no longer knew anyone . . . *after the flesh,* as the apostle says.
And I am going to write my book.

How changed, my soul! how changed!
You once wept but now you smile.
Do not study yourself—explain nothing—let sentiment rule; and then—forge ahead. . . . All things have been renewed. . . .

I said to my soul:
"Why are you smiling? You are hopeless in your solitude. It is as if your erstwhile friend no longer existed. You will have to cease your adulterous dreams.
"Weep. They are gone, all your loved ones, and have left you alone. Weep. Your loves have ended. The time for love is over. . . ."
"Do you believe this?" my soul replied, still smiling and repeating to itself:

Love transcends mourning and death. Acute sorrows have been blotted out and the willows are silent.
Sing, my soul, to new dawns.
All hopes have blossomed anew.